躍變・龍城——九龍城主題步行徑｜社區繪本 08（九龍城篇）

Kowloon City in Transformation – Kowloon City Themed Walking Trail | Picture Book No.8: Kowloon City

繪本名稱：泰好玩
Thai Fun

編輯：北向惠理、周嘉晴
Edited by Kitamukai Eri, Kylie Chow

插畫：唐嘉儀
Illustrated by Yuki Tong

設計排版：唐嘉儀、林紫茵、羅美齡
Designed by Yuki Tong, Traci Lam, Amelia Loh

編審：陳詠琳、鄭詠恩
Reviewed by Gwyneth Chan, Vivian Cheng

督印人：何穎儀
Supervised by Joyce Ho

鳴謝：陳彩蓮（泰二代）
Acknowledged by Chan Choi Lin Vita
(The second generation of Thai)

策劃及出版：躍變・龍城——九龍城主題步行徑
Published by Kowloon City Themed Walking Trail

出版者：萬里機構出版有限公司
Published by Wan Li Book Company Limited

發行：香港聯合書刊物流有限公司
Issued by SUP Publishing Logistics Hong Kong Limited

承印：中華商務彩色印刷有限公司
Printed by C&C Offset Printing Co., Ltd

印量：1,000
1,000 copies in print

出版日期：2024年6月初版
First edition June 2024

九龍城主題步行徑辦公室 Office：
九龍馬頭涌真善美村低座一樓
1/F, Lower Block, Chun Seen Mei Chuen,
Ma Tau Chung, Kowloon

躍變・龍城體驗館 Information Centre：
九龍譚公道115號運通大廈地下5號舖
Shop No.5, Ground Floor, Wan Tung Building,
No.115 Tam Kung Road, Kowloon

電話 Tel：+852 3183 0928
電郵 Email：kctwt@skhwc.org.hk
傳真 Fax：+852 3104 9911
網址 Website：kowlooncitywalkingtrail.hk

🅵 九龍城主題步行徑
🅸 Kowloon City Walking Trail

國際書號 ISBN：978-962-14-7556-5
定價 Price：HK$78.00

步行徑於2022年底舉辦九龍城泰潮文化繪本插畫師招募計劃，並協助兩位獲選的插畫師完成繪本創作、出版及發行，以文字及插畫細訴九龍城的泰潮故事，連繫社區。

At the end of 2022, Kowloon City Themed Walking Trail organised a recruitment programme of illustrators for the Kowloon City Thai and Teochew Culture Picture Book. Two illustrators were selected and provided with assistance in creating, publishing and distributing the picture books. The programme aimed to engage with the community by narrating the Thai and Teochew stories of Kowloon City through words and illustrations.

泰好玩
Thai Fun

主辦 Organised by

躍變●龍城
Kowloon City in Transformation

營運 Operated by

香港聖公會福利協會
HONG KONG SHENG KUNG HUI WELFARE COUNCIL

贊助 Funded by

市區更新基金
Urban Renewal Fund

一日，小玲經過一間泰國雜貨店，
被門前的花環吸引着！

One day, Siu Ling passed by a Thai grocery store and was drawn to the floral garland at the entrance!

泰國人吃水果時喜歡配以這個必備的靈魂醬汁，
試試看吧!

Thai people like adding this essential signature sauce when eating fruits. Give it a try!

是甜甜辣辣的!

It is sweet and spicy!

塗上白色粉末有甚麼意思嗎？

What's the meaning of applying white powder?

新年我們會把白色粉末或粉漿塗抹在對方身上，祝福平安順利。

On New Year's Day, people smear each other's body with white powder symbolising the wish for peace and good fortune.

今天玩得真盡興！
I had a lot of fun today!

我也是。
Me too.

謝謝你邀請我來體驗泰國新年。這是我親手造的香花環。
"Sa-wâd-dee-pee-mâi"！
Thank you for inviting me to experience Thai New Year. This is my hand-made incense garland for you. "Sa-wâd-dee-pee-mâi"！

你甚麼時侯學的？你也「新年快樂」喔~
When did you learn it? "Happy New Year" to you too!

泰式醬汁
Thai Sauce

泰式醬料是泰國美食的靈魂所在，泰國人也會自己調配或調製獨家靈魂醬汁。

Thai sauces are the soul of Thai cuisine and Thai people often prepare their own sauces.

泰國芳香產品
Thai Fragrant Products

泰國人日常生活也會使用不同種類的香氛產品。它們多以天然物料製成，香氣濃厚也是其特色之一。

Thai people like using various scented products in their lives. These products are often made from natural materials and are strongly aromatic.

泰式花環
Thai Floral Garlands

由鮮花和葉製成，是泰國的特色手工藝品。花環代表心意，常用於迎賓、拜見父母長輩、供佛和節日。

Made from fresh flowers and leaves, they are distinctive handicrafts of Thailand. Floral garlands represent gratitude and are often used to welcome guests, greet parents and elders and serve as an offering to the Buddha, or during festivals.

泰國服飾
Thai Clothing

泰國服飾較多採用鮮艷奪目的染料。衣服充滿各種圖案及色彩。

Brilliant-coloured dyes are widely used on Thai clothing. Clothes are full of patterns and colours.

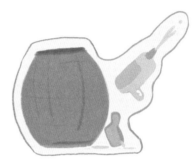

泰國新年(潑水節)
Songkran Festival

新年是泰國人最重視的節日，泰國人會互相潑水及在身體上抹上白色粉末，祈求新一年的好運及平安。

Thai New Year is the most important festival for Thai people. They splash water and apply white powder onto each other to wish for peace and good fortune for the new year.

泰國掛飾
Thai Traditional Decorations

除了美觀，泰國人喜歡風吹動掛飾撞碰發出的聲響。

Apart from aesthetics, Thai people also enjoy the sound made by traditional decorations knocking against each other when the wind blows.

泰國水果雕刻 Thai Fruit Carvings

泰國傳統手藝之一。起源於泰國水燈節，原為泰國宮廷表演的手藝。

One of the distinctive handicrafts in Thailand. Originated from the Loy Krathong Festival, it was an art performance at the Royal Palace.

香港的小泰國
Little Thailand in Hong Kong

九龍城有「小泰國」之稱，其原因最早可以追溯到 1970 年代。許多泰國商人移遷到香港，當中有不少祖籍潮州的華僑，因此選擇落戶於較多潮州人聚居及鄰近舊啟德機場的九龍城。後來，越來越多泰國人來港發展及潮州人迎娶泰裔女子，令九龍城的泰國人口不斷上升。這些泰裔以最拿手的泰國菜為謀生工具，開設泰國雜貨及泰國菜館，令九龍城形成了泰國人集中之地。

而每年四月，這裏都會舉行泰國的傳統新年活動「潑水節」，互相潑水慶祝新年，讓身處在香港的泰國人有一個聚集的機會，也吸引市民前來認識「小泰國」。我們期望透過此繪本，讓小朋友深入淺出了解一些小泰國的文化，同時令這種獨有文化得以承傳。

Kowloon City has long been known as "Little Thailand". This can be traced back to many Thai merchants who migrated to Hong Kong in the 1970s. Some of them were from Teochew, and they chose to settle in Kowloon City, an area with a significant Teochew population and proximity to the old Kai Tak Airport. Over time, the Thai population in Kowloon City increased due to more Thais coming to Hong Kong for opportunities and Teochew people marrying Thai women. These Thai residents, skilled in Thai cuisine, set up Thai grocery stores and restaurants, turning Kowloon City into a focal point.

Every April, the traditional Thai New Year event known as the "Songkran Festival" takes place here, where people splash water onto each other for celebration. This is not only for Thai people in Hong Kong to gather but also a chance for other people to come and find out more about "Little Thailand" in Hong Kong. Through this picture book, we hope to provide children with an idea of Little Thailand's culture in an easily understandable manner, promoting the inheritance of this unique cultural heritage.

躍變‧龍城——
九龍城主題步行徑

由市區更新基金資助,躍變‧龍城——九龍城主題步行徑於2018年1月1日起正式營運,為期7年,步行徑全長約6.5公里,分為5個特色路段,北端以九龍寨城公園為起點,途經宋皇臺、土瓜灣,連接南端的紅磡聖母堂。項目團隊透過改善及美化路段上的硬件設施、舉辦活動、設立訪客中心等連結區內的居民及持份者,以延續及推廣九龍城區的文化歷史。

步行徑社區繪本

步行徑出版一系列繪本,分為九龍城、土瓜灣、紅磡三個篇章,讓區內的幼稚園學生及家長認識社區。我們希望讀者透過繪本,了解步行徑不同路段的歷史文化,並認識步行徑上不同公共設施的硬件知識。

香港聖公會福利協會

聖公會始於1843年。其後,聖公會已在九龍城區興建聖堂與學校,提供社會服務,照顧老弱孤幼,至今180多年,見證社區變化。1966年,香港聖公會福利協會成立,專責提供社會服務。「躍變‧龍城——九龍城主題步行徑」為福利協會近年的重點項目,延續聖公會對九龍城的承擔與情懷。

Kowloon City in Transformation –
Kowloon City Themed Walking Trail

Supported by the Urban Renewal Fund, the 7–year Kowloon City Themed Walking Trail project began operation on 1st January, 2018. The 6.5 km Walking Trail is divided into 5 routes with different characteristics, stretching from Kowloon Walled City Park to its north, and St Mary's Church in Hung Hom to its south. The Walking Trail team has renewed and upgraded various hardware facilities, organised activities and set up an information centre to connect with residents and stakeholders, for continuing and promoting the history of Kowloon City.

Picture Books on the Walking Trail

The Walking Trail publishes a series of picture books of Kowloon City, To Kwa Wan and Hung Hom for students and parents of kindergartens in the districts. With these books, we hope to help readers understand the history and culture of different sections of the walking trail, and learn about its public facilities and hardware.

Hong Kong Sheng Kung Hui Welfare Council

Sheng Kung Hui started its presence in Hong Kong in 1843, soon, Sheng Kung Hui established churches and schools in Kowloon City, providing social services and taking care of the elderly, people in need and orphans. It had been witnessing changes in the community for 180 years. In 1966, Hong Kong Sheng Kung Hui Welfare Council was established to provide social services particularly. Kowloon City in Transformation – Kowloon City Themed Walking Trail is a key project of the Welfare Council in recent years, continuing Sheng Kung Hui's love and care for Kowloon City.